Dear Parents and Educators,

Welcome to Penguin Young Readers! As parents and educators, you know that each child develops at his or her own pace—in terms of speech, critical thinking, and, of course, reading. Penguin Young Readers recognizes this fact. As a result, each Penguin Young Readers book is assigned a traditional easy-to-read level (1–4) as well as a Guided Reading Level (A–P). Both of these systems will help you choose the right book for your child. Please refer to the back of each book for specific leveling information. Penguin Young Readers features esteemed authors and illustrators, stories about favorite characters, fascinating nonfiction, and more!

| Oliver and Amanda More Tales of Amanda Pig | LEVEL **3** GUIDED READING LEVEL **L** |

This book is perfect for a **Transitional Reader** who:
• can read multisyllable and compound words;
• can read words with prefixes and suffixes;
• is able to identify story elements (beginning, middle, end, plot, setting, characters, problem, solution); and
• can understand different points of view.

Here are some **activities** you can do during and after reading this book:
• On a separate sheet of paper, make a list of all the words in the story that have an -ed ending. Then write the root word next to the word with the -ed ending. The chart below will get you started.

| word with an -ed ending | root word |
|---|---|
| asked | ask |

• Comprehension: Answer the following questions after reading the story.
  • In "Mother and Father," what did Amanda and Oliver learn about being parents?
  • Discuss how Amanda felt in the story "Company." What did she do about it?

Remember, sharing the love of reading with a child is the best gift you can give!

—Bonnie Bader, EdM
  Penguin Young Readers program

*Penguin Young Readers are leveled by independent reviewers applying the standards developed by Irene Fountas and Gay Su Pinnell in *Matching Books to Readers: Using Leveled Books in Guided Reading*, Heinemann, 1999.

For Elizabeth who, when she grows up,
will never ever eat eggs—JVL

For Anne Schwartz and Atha Tehon—AS

Penguin Young Readers
Published by the Penguin Group
Penguin Group (USA) Inc., 375 Hudson Street, New York, New York 10014, USA
Penguin Group (Canada), 90 Eglinton Avenue East, Suite 700, Toronto, Ontario M4P 2Y3, Canada
(a division of Pearson Penguin Canada Inc.)
Penguin Books Ltd, 80 Strand, London WC2R 0RL, England
Penguin Ireland, 25 St Stephen's Green, Dublin 2, Ireland (a division of Penguin Books Ltd)
Penguin Group (Australia), 707 Collins Street, Melbourne, Victoria 3008, Australia
(a division of Pearson Australia Group Pty Ltd)
Penguin Books India Pvt Ltd, 11 Community Centre, Panchsheel Park, New Delhi—110 017, India
Penguin Group (NZ), 67 Apollo Drive, Rosedale, Auckland 0632, New Zealand
(a division of Pearson New Zealand Ltd)
Penguin Books (South Africa), Rosebank Office Park, 181 Jan Smuts Avenue,
Parktown North 2193, South Africa
Penguin China, B7 Jiaming Center, 27 East Third Ring Road North,
Chaoyang District, Beijing 100020, China

Penguin Books Ltd, Registered Offices: 80 Strand, London WC2R 0RL, England

Text copyright © 1985 by Jean Van Leeuwen. Illustrations copyright © 1985 by Ann Schweninger.
All rights reserved. First published in 1985 and 1988 by Dial Books for Young Readers, an imprint of
Penguin Group (USA) Inc. Published in 1995 in a Puffin Easy-to-Read edition. Published in 2013 by
Penguin Young Readers, an imprint of Penguin Group (USA) Inc., 345 Hudson Street,
New York, New York 10014. Manufactured in China.

The Library of Congress has cataloged the Dial edition under
the following Control Number: 84028775

ISBN 978-0-14-037603-6                    10 9 8 7 6 5 4 3 2

# Oliver and Amanda

# More Tales of Amanda Pig

by Jean Van Leeuwen
pictures by Ann Schweninger

Penguin Young Readers
An Imprint of Penguin Group (USA) Inc.

# Contents

# Chapter 1
## Mother and Father

"Father," said Amanda.

"What is it?" asked Father.

"I'm talking to Oliver," said Amanda. "He is the father. You are the grandfather."

"I see," said Father.

"Father," said Amanda, "our baby is hungry, and there is no food in the house. Will you go to the store?"

"Yes, Mother," said Oliver.

"What did you say?" asked Mother.

"I'm talking to Amanda," said Oliver. "You are the grandmother."

Oliver came back with a big bag of food.

"Our baby keeps crying," said Amanda. "I think she has a temperature. Will you hold her, Father?"

Amanda gave Oliver the baby. Oliver gave Amanda the bag of food. She dropped it on the floor.

"Oh dear," she said. "Now we have to sweep the floor."

Oliver and Amanda swept the floor.

"Amanda, I mean Mother," said Oliver. "I think I hear the other babies crying."

"What other babies?" asked Amanda.

"Our other babies," said Oliver. "I will go check."

He came back with the other babies.

"They are all sick," he said. "They have a hundred and two."

"Oh dear," said Amanda. "I better call the doctor."

"Yes, Doctor," she said. "I will give them the pink medicine. I have to hang up now. The spaghetti and meatballs are burning on the stove."

Amanda hung up.

"Oh dear," she said. "Our dinner is all burned up."

"Never mind," said Oliver. "I will cook banana pancakes."

Amanda gave the babies the pink medicine.

"I think they are feeling better," she said.

"Dinner is ready," said Oliver.
Oliver and Amanda and all the
babies sat down at the table.

"Don't talk with your mouth full,
Sallie Rabbit," said Amanda.

"Tiger, stop throwing food at Elephant," said Oliver.

"These babies have no manners at all," said Amanda. "Oh dear. Now look what Sallie Rabbit did."

"What did she do?" asked Oliver.

"Spilled her milk," said Amanda. "All over everything."

"We better get the mop," said
Oliver.

They went to the kitchen.

"Grandmother," said Amanda.
"May we have juice and cookies? We
are all tired out."

"It's the babies," said Oliver.

"How many babies do you have?" asked Mother.

"Twelve," said Amanda.

"You better sit down and rest," said Mother.

Oliver and Amanda rested.

Mother got the juice and cookies.

"Being a mother and father is hard work," said Amanda.

"It certainly is," said Mother.

"Mother," said Oliver. "Do you hear a baby crying?"

Amanda listened.

She took another bite of cookie.

"I don't hear a thing," she said.

# Chapter 2
## Company

"Why are you cooking and cooking?" asked Amanda.

"Company is coming," said Mother.

"Who is the company?" asked
Amanda.

"Your aunt Sara and uncle Mort,"
said Mother. "And your cousins Sam
and Emily and Peter."

Oliver put on his sailor suit.

Amanda put on her sundress.

She dressed Sallie Rabbit in her
best pajamas.

They waited for the company.

"When will they come?" asked Oliver.

"Any minute," said Mother.

"Is it any minute yet?" asked Amanda.

"Here they are," said Father.

Uncle Mort lifted Amanda up high.

"Who is this big girl?" he asked.

"Amanda," said Amanda.

Mother and Father and Aunt Sara and Uncle Mort sat down in the living room.

The cousins went outside.

"What is there to do?" asked Sam.

"Play in my sandbox," said Amanda.

"Sandboxes are for babies," said Sam.

"Play in my fort," said Oliver.

All the cousins went to Oliver's fort.

Amanda built a sand castle alone.

"What can we ride?" asked Sam.

"I have a wagon," said Amanda.

"I have a new bike," said Oliver.

"Oh boy," said Sam. "Let's ride it."

He zoomed all over the yard on Oliver's bike.

After his turn, everyone had a turn.

Except Amanda.

Her feet didn't reach the pedals.

Then they played hide-and-seek.

Sam found Oliver hiding in the
apple tree.

Oliver found Emily hiding in the
sandbox.

No one even looked for Amanda.

"Lunchtime!" called Mother.

Everyone ran to the picnic table under the apple tree.

"Oh boy, lemonade!" said Sam.

"And chocolate cake!" said Oliver.

They pushed and grabbed and laughed.

"This company is too noisy," said Amanda.

She took Sallie Rabbit and crawled under the table.

It was dark there.

And quiet.

And there were a lot of feet.

"It's like a little house," said Amanda.

"It's a cave," said someone.

It was her cousin Peter.

"We could pretend it's a cave house," said Amanda.

"We could," said Peter.

"I have a rabbit," said Amanda. "Her name is Sallie Rabbit."

"I have an alligator," said Peter. "His name is Alligator."

Then Amanda and Peter had a picnic in their cave house.

They ate chocolate cake and listened to the noisy company and counted feet and picked up cake crumbs. And Sallie Rabbit and Alligator ate every one.

# Chapter 3
## The Bubble Bath

"Just look at you, Sallie Rabbit,"
said Amanda. "You've got egg on
your chin and grape ice pop on your
paws and mud on your stomach.
What a mess."

"Tiger has four stripes on his stomach," said Oliver. "And seven spots."

"What these babies need is a bath," said Amanda.

Oliver ran water in the bathtub. Amanda poured in some bubble bath.

"Okay, Sallie Rabbit," she said. "Start scrubbing. I will help you."

Amanda worked on Sallie's stomach. She scrubbed and scrubbed.

"Sorry, Sallie," she said. "This is hard dirt. We need more soap."

She poured in some shampoo.

"I can't get the bubble gum out of Tiger's tail," said Oliver.

He poured in more bubble bath.

"Oops!" He dropped in the whole bottle by mistake.

"Oh well," said Amanda. "Our babies will get really clean."

Bubbles rose in the air. Bubbles spilled over the bathtub and covered the floor.

"Uh-oh," said Amanda.

She couldn't see Sallie Rabbit. She couldn't even see the bathtub.

Bubbles were creeping out the door and into the hall.

"Help!" called Amanda.

Mother came upstairs.

"Amanda! Oliver! Where are you?"

"Here," said Amanda. "In all these bubbles."

"What should we do?" asked Oliver.

"Let the water out of the tub," said Mother.

"I can't find the tub," said Oliver.

"I'll do it," said Mother.

But she slipped and slid and landed on the floor.

"Ouch!" cried Oliver. "You just found me."

"And me," said Amanda.

Slowly the bubbles started to melt.

Amanda could see the bathtub
again.

And Mother's face.

It was angry.

"Just look at this mess," she said.
"How could you make such a mess?
And look at you."

Amanda looked at Oliver.

"You look like a clown," she said.

"You look like a cloud," said
Oliver. "And look at Mother. She
looks like she is wearing a hat."

They looked in the mirror.

Mother laughed.

"I like my new hat," she said.

"I like my new nose," said Oliver.

They all laughed.

Then they started cleaning up.

Oliver and Amanda wrapped
Sallie Rabbit and Tiger in towels.

"Look, Mother," said Amanda.
"Our babies are clean."

"So they are," said Mother. "But
no more bubble baths for a while."

Amanda blew a bubble out
of Sallie Rabbit's ear.

"Did you hear that, Sallie?" she
said. "No more bubble baths."

# Chapter 4
## The Birthday Present

"Today is somebody's birthday," said Mother.

"Is it my birthday?" asked Amanda.

"No," said Mother. "You just had your birthday."

"I want it to be my birthday again," said Amanda. "So I can get bigger and bigger."

"It's not my birthday," said Oliver.

"No," said Mother. "Yours is soon, but today is Father's birthday."

"Let's have a party," said Amanda.

"Good idea," said Mother. "What shall we have for the party?"

"Birthday cake," said Amanda.

"Ice cream," said Oliver.

"Balloons," said Amanda.

"Party hats," said Oliver.

"And a present," said Mother.

She took a box out of the closet.

Oliver and Amanda looked inside.

"Father doesn't wear short pants," said Oliver.

"It's a bathing suit," said Mother.

"I want to give Father a present," said Oliver. "But I can't buy one."

"Me too," said Amanda.

"A present doesn't need to be something you buy," said Mother. "It can be anything at all that you think Father would like."

Oliver went to his room.

"Father would like this," he said. "It's a very round rock."

"What a nice present," said Mother. "I will help you wrap it up."

Amanda went to her room.

She looked at all her toys.

"Father is too big for blocks," she said. "And he has his own car. What could be a present for Father?"

She saw Sallie Rabbit sitting on her bed.

"If I were Father," she said, "this is what I would like for my birthday."

She picked her up.

"But I like Sallie, too," she said.

She put her down.

"But it would be the very best birthday present," she said.

Father liked his birthday party.

He liked all his presents.

"Something to wear and
something to hold and something
to hug," he said. "Thank you,
everyone."

Later Amanda lay in her bed.

She couldn't sleep.

Her bed felt wide and empty
without Sallie Rabbit.

Father opened the door.

"Amanda," he said, "I can't
sleep. It's Sallie Rabbit. She keeps
wiggling."

"She never wiggles when she sleeps with me," said Amanda.

"Maybe she misses you," said Father.

"Well, I am her mother," said Amanda.

"I think she still needs a mother," said Father.

"Would you mind taking care of her for me until she is a little bigger?"

"I wouldn't mind," said Amanda.

"Thank you," said Father.

Amanda hugged Sallie Rabbit tight.

"Good night, Father," she said. "Good night, Sallie Rabbit."

# Chapter 5
## Growing Up

"Mother," said Amanda. "What can I help you do?"

"You can help mix up these muffins for dinner," said Mother.

Amanda helped mix up the
muffins.

"What a good helper you are
getting to be," said Mother.

"I can do a lot of things," said
Amanda. "I am almost grown up,
you know. Soon I will be moving out."

"Oh my," said Mother. "Already? Come and tell me more about it while we wait for Father and Oliver."

Mother and Amanda sat in the big chair.

"What do you think you will do when you grow up?" asked Mother.

"I will be a ballet dancer," said Amanda. "And a cook and a doctor and I will fly to the moon."

"All at once?" said Mother. "You will be busy."

"I am going to be very busy when I grow up," said Amanda.

"Where will you live," asked Mother, "when you are not on the moon?"

"I will build a house next door to you," said Amanda.

"And I will do whatever I want whenever I want to do it. I will wear perfume all the time and go to bed at midnight and never eat eggs."

"That sounds good," said Mother. "Will you have any babies?"

"Maybe six," said Amanda.

"I wonder what I will look like
when I grow up. Will I look like you?"

"Maybe," said Mother. "But mostly
I think you will look just like yourself.
And I will miss you."

"Don't worry," said Amanda.
"I will still come to see you. On
Mondays and Fridays."

"That will be good," said Mother. "Will we still sit in the big chair?"

"I don't think so," said Amanda. "I think I will be too big to fit."

"Oh dear," said Mother. "I will really miss that. We had better hug now before it is too late."

They had a big hug.

"Mother," said Amanda. "Maybe I won't get so very big when I grow up. Maybe we will still fit."

"I hope so," said Mother.

And they had another big hug in the big chair waiting for Father and Oliver.